The bird raised its wings as if to attack. Spread like that it was huge and Solomon was afraid. He wobbled, but he was not going to turn back now. He glared back at the owl with equal determination.

Then something happened which made everything – even the danger he was in – worthwhile. From the space at the other end of the beam, two small faces peeped out and squeaked plaintively. They were magical: little balls of white fluff with round faces, as curious to see Solomon as he was to see them.

HIPPO ANIMAL

Owl Cry

Deborah van der Beek

Hippo

for Andrew

Scholastic Children's Books,
Commonwealth House, 1–19 New Oxford Street,
London WC1A 1NU, UK
a division of Scholastic Ltd
London ~ New York ~ Toronto ~ Sydney ~ Auckland

First published by Scholastic Ltd, 1997

Text copyright © Deborah van der Beek, 1997

ISBN 0 590 19532 8

Typeset by TW Typesetting, Midsomer Norton, Somerset

Printed and bound in Great Britain by
Caledonian International Book Manufacturing Ltd, Glasgow

10 9 8 7 6 5 4 3 2 1

The author would like to thank Ashley Smith at the Hawk Conservatory Trust, Andover, and Barney and Freda Owl at Lackham College, Chippenham.

Chapter 1

In the blackness a last flame flickered and died. Moments before, hot fierce fire had bellowed angrily in a stink of smoke. Now there was nothing.

Out of the dark a white shape floated noiselessly on to the road: it had seen something move.

The heap of twisted metal lay dull red in a smash of melted glass and plastic. But across the road, something stirred in a pile of rags.

A mouse? The owl leaned forward, ready to pounce. In the rags two bright eyes opened, blinked and stared into the two fierce ones. It was no mouse.

The owl gave a "huff" of alarm and spread her wings to land back a step. But she was not really scared. She put her head on one side and inspected the bundle from all angles. Then she strutted up and down, chucking to herself softly while the eyes followed her this way and that.

The creature in the bundle sat up to see the owl better. It had a huge head for a body no larger than the owl itself. Brown eyes glowed in the thin, dirty face.

"Aah!" it said, and stretched out a grubby paw. This was too much for the owl. Still silent, on silent wings it took flight and left. The baby let out a heart-rending wail of sorrow and disappointment.

It was hours before a passing motorist screeched to a shocked halt and carried the baby, still sobbing, into the nearest police station.

Staff-nurse Harvey, mother of four, held out her arms. The young policeman heaved a sigh of relief. "It stinks!" he warned.

Staff-nurse Harvey gave him a withering look. "Of course it – he – does," she said, unwrapping the little creature with kind hands. But even she was shocked. How thin he was! How red and sore with dirt.

"Poor love," she murmured. "He looks like a baby bird."

In a jokey way they called the baby Solomon: the solemn eyes in the too-thin face were what everyone noticed first.

Solomon spent his first years in various Children's Homes in London. He wasn't adopted, as most babies would be, because the police hoped someone would turn up for him. But no one did. Who were his parents? It remained a mystery. Were they the two bodies found in the wrecked car? If they were, they hadn't looked after him well. He was under-weight and far too small for a baby of fourteen months.

Solomon stayed small and thin, eyes suspicious under a mop of black hair. By the time he was eight years old, he was getting mixed up in things he shouldn't. Solomon was nimble too, and some of the older boys in the Home found this only too useful…

*   *   *

Those who planned the burglaries had to admire the cool daring of someone who shinned up a drainpipe and scuttled along the highest roofs without fear.

"Where is he?" voices would whisper from below.

"Why's he so slow?"

"Don't fret. Sol'll be all right." Gavin Bratley was always about on these occasions and very much the leader. He had been in the Home almost as long as Solomon. Gavin was four years older than Solomon, and the first to see what might be done by being nice to the skinny monkey.

Once inside Solomon would take his time, going from room to room. He saw tidy houses and untidy houses with unmade beds and clothes left in crumpled heaps on the floor. The children's rooms were the messiest. Sometimes Solomon picked a toy up and looked at it. He wondered about the person it belonged to. What would it be like to be that person? Then he would race downstairs to let the others in.

"Told you so," Gavin would say as Solomon opened the door. And he would clap Solomon on the back and wink. "Brilliant bloke, Sol." Gavin didn't say things like that to everyone.

When he was ten, something happened to change Solomon's life.

"We've found a nice family who want to adopt you." Solomon's new social worker was big and plump. There was a smudge of bright red lipstick on the side of her mouth, because she had a nervous habit of rubbing it with her finger. Her dress was long and flowery.

Solomon decided she was stupid. He liked his old social worker, Pam. Why did Pam have to move? It was always the same in the Home – you got to know someone and then they moved away, or got another job.

"Yes, Miss Bucket," he said.

Miss Birkett looked at him. Did he know he'd got her name wrong again? She wasn't sure. She said hesitantly, "You can call me Jenny, if you like."

"Yes, Miss."

"It's in the country."

"The country?" Solomon stared. The smudge reached almost to her chin now.

"We thought you needed a – a fresh start." She looked at him pointedly.

Solomon hung his head: he liked Gavin Bratley, but he wasn't proud of getting mixed up in stealing.

"It's just a try-out at first. To see how you all get on. But I think you'll like Sonia and William Oakley. Pam told me they're terribly nice. They have no other children. They've been waiting ages to adopt."

What she didn't say was that this couple were thought to be particularly suitable because the wife was a child psychologist and an old school friend of Pam Dexter's.

Solomon didn't know if he wanted to go or not. At least he did – terribly – but suppose it all went wrong? And what would Gavin say? He picked a ball from his pocket and began bouncing it up and down.

Miss Birkett waited. In the end she said, "Well, are you going to give it a go?"

Solomon gave it a few more minutes. Then he said, "Do I get my own room?"

Miss Birkett was sure of that one. "Oh, yes."

Solomon said nothing. Then he shrugged. "OK, Miss Bucket."

Chapter 2

The garden gate was painted blue. The paint was bubbled in places, and a faded sign on it read "Screech Cottage: BEWARE OF THE DOG".

Solomon gulped nervously. No matter what he'd told Miss Birkett, he was dead scared: it was a moment he had been waiting for all his life. A proper family! Just think of it: a father, and – more than anything else – a real live mother; his very own and nobody else's.

Miss Birkett opened the gate and called, "Sonia?"

Solomon, behind her, saw a plain pebble-dash house with blue paintwork and the sort of garden that is mostly dry earth with sad clumps of vegetables dotted here and there.

At that moment Solomon nearly turned round and jumped right back in the car. Then he thought of what Gavin Bratley would say if he was so pathetic. Anyway, he was only here for the weekend. Miss Birkett had told him a hundred times: "You can change your mind at any time. The adoption papers won't be signed until we're sure it's what you all want." Solomon did want. Very much.

Miss Birkett called again, more timidly. "Sonia – Mrs Oakley?"

Solomon noticed a black labrador lying in a basket by the door. It got up and growled at them nastily. Miss Birkett backed into Solomon, hurting his foot badly. She was very heavy. Solomon scowled.

"What?" A man came round from the back of the house.

"Ah, Mr Oakley?" The man nodded and frowned. He was short, with stubby fair hair and a crumpled red face. He looked very tired, as if he hadn't slept all night, or as if he'd just woken up.

"Yes?" It wasn't a very friendly welcome.

"This is Solomon," Miss Birkett said.

"Oh! But—" A look of complete astonishment came over the man's face. "Oh!"

Solomon's excitement sucked away like water down a plughole. What was wrong? This had all been planned for weeks and weeks. And where was the mother? Solomon looked all round, behind the man and into all the windows of the house. Perhaps she was inside? But no one appeared.

The man gave him a crooked smile that looked a bit stuck on. Solomon didn't give one back.

Miss Birkett was still nervously watching the dog, which stood with its head low, waiting. Every now and then the sides of its mouth lifted and a deep growl came out like distant thunder.

"Back, Josie – basket." The dog sniffed crossly, and stumped back to its place by the door.

Miss Birkett burbled on about this and that… "I'm Jenny Birkett. I've taken over from Pam Dexter. I've spoken to your wife on the phone a great deal."

"Yes…"

"And where is Mrs Oakley … does she know we've arrived?"

"Sonia? … Ye-es." The man hesitated. Then he seemed to decide. "She's out, I'm afraid." He spoke to Miss Birkett, but kept giving Solomon little sneaky looks.

Solomon didn't like it. It was the mother he wanted to meet. It was the mother he'd thought about, night after night. Sonia sounded such a soft, lovely name. Why wasn't she here? His chest felt tight with disappointment. To his horror, he found his eyes becoming damp.

He looked fiercely at the ground.

"Out? But this has been arranged for ages. I spoke to her only last week." Miss Birkett sounded very disapproving.

There was a pause. Then Mr Oakley said, "She had to go. It was a funeral – a long way away. She won't be back this weekend."

Something about the way he said it made Solomon think: he's not telling the truth. But that didn't make sense. Why should he lie?

"A funeral? Oh – I am sorry." Miss Birkett was embarrassed. "I hope it wasn't anyone close?" She looked worried. "Oh dear, I don't know what I should do … maybe I should just take him back." Her large bosom heaved like a flower-bed in a breeze.

"He'll be all right," said the man.

"I don't mind," Solomon said stiffly. It seemed rude to say anything else – it would look as if he didn't believe Oakley. But he did mind. He wished Miss Birkett would look at him. Surely she'd see he didn't want to stay? Not if the mother wasn't there.

But Miss Birkett had her nose deep in her papers.

"Oh dear," she said again. "I wonder if there's anything in the rules..." If Sonia hadn't been an old friend of Pam's she would have taken him back without hesitation ... it made things very difficult.

William Oakley ignored her. "I'll take this," he said, and, picking up Solomon's case, led them inside. A few minutes later Miss Birkett left, rather fast, with Josie's nose stuck firmly into her backside.

Safe behind the gate she called: "Just the weekend, then. I'll be back Sunday night."

The sound of her car died away. They turned to looked at each other. William Oakley frowned: he didn't seem to know what to do, what to say to this skinny little shrimp who was scowling at him so angrily.

"I – I'll show you round," he said gruffly. Solomon nodded and followed Oakley up narrow stairs.

"This is your room." Solomon had barely time to look in, before William Oakley had dumped his case and moved on.

"Bathroom's there ... and that's where I sleep. Josie isn't allowed upstairs. She'll get used to you." The dog had appeared again at the foot of the stairs. Solomon shrank back, for she showed no sign of friendship. Her grey snout was wrinkled in silent warning.

"Living-room, television … kitchen … um … That's it." William Oakley came to an awkward halt. He muttered something about supper and disappeared. Solomon wondered if he should help. But when he came to the kitchen door, Oakley's back was towards him and he didn't dare speak.

He switched the television on and sat without watching it. He noticed Oakley had said "that's where I sleep": surely the usual thing was to say "our bedroom"? It was all very odd.

Supper was uncomfortably silent. William Oakley tried to make conversation, but it was rather hard with Solomon glaring at him. Soon he gave up. "Maybe it'll be better in the morning," Oakley told himself.

But Solomon was fighting tears. This was supposed to be the best thing that had ever happened to him and it had gone wrong from the very start. As soon as he dared, Solomon excused himself and went upstairs.

At least one thing was right – his room. His very own room! He couldn't wait to tell Gavin. It was not a very big one. It was square, with a low ceiling and a window that stuck up out of the roof. There was a new wooden desk, and a pin-board with brochures from a local swimming pool, sports centre and one or two other things. Above the bed was a poster of a young fox in a ferny wood.

But Solomon was too disappointed to be really pleased. And what would Gavin say now? "Yah! Told you so – things are never what they tell you." Tight with misery, he undressed and got into bed. He didn't bother to unpack. Once, he heard footsteps outside in the passage. The door opened and closed very quietly. Solomon pretended he was asleep.

Much later he was jerked awake by a loud noise. It had come from somewhere quite close by – possibly even the next room. What was it? It sounded like a scream. Solomon froze.

The scream came again. Someone – it sounded like a woman – was being hurt. Who could it be?

In his long years in the Home, Solomon had heard many tales of violence in the family: he knew it could, and often did, happen. Suddenly, with a gulp of fear, Solomon knew: it must, could only be – Sonia!

Quickly, he pieced things together in his mind. It all fitted only too well: Oakley really had been lying, Sonia was not away at all. She had been here all the time, locked in a cellar or somewhere she couldn't cry for help. And now? Now Oakley was murdering her.

Solomon's first thoughts were for Sonia. He must rescue her! But how? A skinny child like him was no match for the burly Oakley. If he went for help it would be too late. Anyway, who would believe him – a boy already in trouble with the police?

Then Solomon realized something else. And that something made the hairs on his back stand up and ripple down like the fin on a fish. His mouth went dry at the very thought.

He, Solomon, could be next to be murdered... In fact, why else had Oakley been so keen to keep him? He was alone in a house with a madman and murderer.

All these thoughts whirled through Solomon's mind. Quickly he felt for his clothes in the dark.

Another scream came. It was a cry of agony, of long, drawn-out pain. Solomon was trembling so much he could hardly think straight. He tried to calm himself, to be sensible. What should he do? How could he get away? He dared not go through the house – even if Oakley didn't hear him, the old dog would. Luckily, the window presented no problems to an experienced climber like Solomon. With feverish fingers he tore back the curtains and flung it wide.

Then it was as if in the middle of a horror video he had switched channels to a silent film … something astonishing and different.

A cold moon shone. He saw a huge, pale bird – an owl – perched on the roof so close he might have touched it. Smoothly its head turned to stare at him, the black, glossy eyes

piercing and perfect in the round face. It screamed again.

Solomon gasped, and in dreamlike slow motion the owl shaped wordless white wings for flight. But even as it rose the proud eyes never left Solomon's own. In these split seconds he took in the snowy pillow of its breast. He saw how precise was the patterning of droplets and lace, black and white on the gold of its back.

Something stirred deep in Solomon. He'd seen something like that before... What was it? When was it? As he stood at the open window, bits floated in to him, bits half remembered, long forgotten. He was in a car. Angry voices. Smash! A fire ... and then the owl ... he had wanted to touch it, but it had gone.

Solomon burst into tears. He cried for the bad mother long gone, and the new one who hadn't even bothered to turn up. A long time later he closed the window.

Never mind William Oakley. He wanted to see that owl again.

Chapter 3

"**T**yto alba": Barn Owl. Solomon looked at the picture. That was it! It couldn't be anything else. He read the text on the opposite page.

"Alba means white. This owl is the only one of the 'Tyto' family in Britain… Call: an eerie scream" (yes!) … it "doesn't hoot". (Solomon had thought all owls hooted.) "…Nests in holes in old trees, or old buildings." But the book didn't tell him much. "Nest can sometimes be located by the proximity of large number of pellets." What were pellets? They sounded really weird.

Just then, William Oakley came up. Somehow Solomon wanted to keep the owl to himself just now. He put the bird book back quickly and grabbed one on football, which didn't interest him very much.

"Take anything you like – help yourself," Oakley said. "I've got to go and see about some tree planting. You can come if you want."

"No, thank you." Solomon wished Oakley would hurry up and go, so he could look round quietly, on his own.

He had an ambitious plan: he would find all the large, old trees nearby, and climb each one. Then he would try buildings. If he stuck to this – in the end he must surely find the owl.

Oakley scratched his chin. "Oh … well. You can go where you like on the estate. Mr Locke won't mind. I'm sure you know about shutting gates. Don't climb on tractors or go into the hayloft. It's not safe … it's all going to be converted into houses, so Mr Locke isn't bothering with repairs."

Solomon nodded.

Climbing every tree was harder than he had imagined: in the country there were such a lot of them! By the time he had done nine he was fed up. He had grazed his elbow twice in the same place and it was beginning to rain.

Across the fields, a clock chimed twelve. Still an hour before he had to go in for lunch. At that moment, Oakley came by on a tractor. Solomon wanted to call out and ride with him, but Oakley wouldn't hear above the noise of the engine. Instead they exchanged polite smiles.

Something niggled in Solomon's mind; what had Oakley said about a hayloft? Forbidden? Nothing was more likely to appeal to a boy like Solomon. The moment the tractor was gone Solomon headed for it.

The hayloft was a wonderful place to explore. It was large as a church hall and almost as high. On one side, bales reached to a roof criss-crossed with beams. There would be lots of good hiding places – for a boy as well as an owl. Solomon climbed up and up. He squeezed between two bales and kept still. How quiet it was!

He could hear William Oakley on his tractor – a distant road – a cow, all muffled by the hay. Much nearer were tiny scuffles and scratchings: mice. Solomon was still for so long that one even came out: it was much smaller than he'd expected – maybe a baby? It sat on a bale and clasped its tiny paws, ducking its head through them again and again to clean its face.

William Oakley called and the mouse whisked away. Solomon clambered down. In his hurry he put his hand right into a pile of animal droppings – they were not bird, and far too large to belong to the little mouse. Rat-muck! Eugh! Solomon held his polluted hand out, making Oakley ask if he'd hurt it.

"Where have you been? You're filthy," Oakley said, not unkindly.

"Er … nowhere," Solomon mumbled, and dashed off to scrub himself.

That night Solomon listened out for the screams… There they were again. They were further off tonight. He smiled to remember the murderous scenes he had thought up the night before. And when William Oakley came in to say good night, Solomon almost burst into fits of giggles.

Oakley said: "It's a screech owl – a barn owl. Probably more than one; a pair, I expect. That's why this is 'Screech Cottage' – there have always been barn owls here." He added proudly, "I read somewhere that barn owls are quite rare now. We're very lucky to have them here… I came to warn you last night but you were asleep. I hope you weren't worried by it? – Why are you smiling?" But Solomon wouldn't tell him.

As soon as he'd gone Solomon turned the light off and went to the window. A "screech" owl. Well, that suited it all right … and

Screech Cottage. Of course. It sounded much better when you knew it was owls the cottage was named after. And they were quite rare now – that made seeing one even more special.

Why were they rare? he wondered. But Oakley was no longer there to ask. Although Solomon fought off sleep for nearly an hour the owls didn't come any nearer. And he was going back tomorrow.

Chapter 4

M iss Birkett was driving Solomon home. "How was it?"

"OK."

"Just 'OK'? Not good then?"

"What are owl pellets?" Solomon couldn't resist asking.

Miss Birkett nearly ran the car into a wall. "Pardon?"

Solomon wished he'd kept quiet. But a few minutes later Miss Birkett said, "I've remembered! Owl pellets. I worked at a school that did a project on them. Because birds don't have teeth, owls mostly swallow their prey whole. They can't digest the bony bits, so they cough them back up all squashed into pellets.

The schools were asked to find out what the owls ate by pulling the pellets to bits... They look a bit like long, black beans. It sounds horrid, but it isn't really – I didn't know you were interested in birds, Solomon?"

"Me? Oh. I'm not really," Solomon said hastily. "It – it just came up." Suddenly he sat up: black beans. Wouldn't that be the same as those things he'd thought were rat droppings? He had to go back and see.

"Am I going again next weekend?"

"Do you want to?" Miss Birkett asked.

"All right. Yeah."

"Good. And next time," she added brightly, "Sonia will be back. You can have a whole week before I need to do my report. Then we'll really be able to see if you all get on."

Solomon thought back over the silent meals with William Oakley, the awful moments when he arrived. Funny, he'd almost forgotten about Sonia since discovering the owls. Well, it would all be better next week.

Back at the Home it seemed very noisy and busy. The House Mother was caught up with a pair of very rowdy twins who had come to stay while their mother was in hospital. The Home was always like this – people coming and going, fights, shouting. You had to be tough to survive.

Gavin Bratley was going around with a new boy a bit younger than Solomon. He ignored Solomon. As every day passed Solomon looked forward more and more to the weekend.

On Friday, Solomon leapt out of the car and was running to the gate before Miss Birkett had turned off the engine. He heard Oakley's voice: "Basket, Josie – basket!"

He saw Oakley coming towards him, his face still unsmiling. But this time Solomon didn't care. Round the side of the house was a deck-chair. It was facing the other way, and there was someone sitting in it – Sonia! In a moment she would get up and see him. It was going to be all right.

Miss Birkett was still parking the car with a nasty grinding of gears. Parking always took her ages, because she could never quite decide if she were in someone's way or not.

Solomon ran back to her, his face shining. "It's all right – she's back! Sonia's here!"

Miss Birkett turned off the engine and wound down the window. "What? Good. I'll just be a moment. I'm still not quite right yet."

Solomon said, "It's all right. You needn't come in."

"Oh, but I must."

"I don't want you to. I want to meet – my mother – on my own."

"Oh." Miss Birkett looked doubtful. "I'm sure I shouldn't…"

"Go," Solomon insisted. "Please. It's important."

Miss Birkett hesitated. She looked at Solomon's glowing face. He seemed so sure … after all, it was his very special moment. And Pam Dexter had been certain the Oakleys were a suitable couple.

"All right then," she said. "I'll ring."

Solomon ran in again, his heart full of joy. But the deck-chair was empty now. Solomon stood as if rooted and cast his eyes about the garden. There was no one to be seen, though the deck-chair swung slightly as if someone had just left it. Behind him, Oakley closed the gate Solomon had left open in his eagerness.

By the door, Josie watched him in silence, head on paws. And then Solomon realized – it had been Josie in the chair. It had not been Sonia after all.

"Where is she?" he cried. "Where's Sonia?"

William Oakley looked away. And, as Solomon knew he would, he mumbled, "She's not here."

"Where is she then?" Solomon cried again. "When is she coming?"

Then, as Oakley said nothing, he ran off.

Chapter 5

Solomon ran round behind the house, sneaked through the yard and into the hayloft. He wanted to be somewhere quiet, somewhere Oakley wouldn't find him.

Something was very wrong – he knew it. Why hadn't Sonia come? Why wouldn't Oakley answer him? What was it all about? Solomon pushed up through the hay bales till he was in a place where he couldn't be seen from the ground.

He wasn't thinking of owls at all. But suddenly, way up in the roof, a squawk and a flutter made him look up. A split-second glimpse of a pale wing made him forget everything that had just happened.

It was an owl! It really was – he had found one. He didn't stop to think if the owl might mind him looking. All he cared was that one was there and he wanted to see closer. As he climbed higher, his excitement mounted. He knew he was going to see it – he just knew.

The bales of hay were stacked up to where beams running across stopped them going any higher. Above that, the roof sloped, so that the beams higher up were much shorter. He could see they were littered with bird messes, and what he had earlier thought to be rat droppings. He picked one up and examined it. It was about five centimetres long and rounded at both ends. It didn't smell at all. He crumbled it between his fingers – it was quite dry. Solomon smiled in triumph as dozens of tiny bones and furry stuff fell into his palm.

Solomon chose his route expertly. It was quite dark here, and some of the cross-beams felt unsafe: he would have to be careful. He was panting from the effort and concentrating hard, when he looked across and saw what he had been waiting for.

Right at the other end of the very beam he sat astride was an owl.

The black eyes glared at him. Solomon's excitement was nearly as fierce: he was wild with it. He had to get closer! How beautiful it was! It hardly seemed real. Its white was so white, and in the half-light the gold on its back shone like polished wood.

Where the beam rested on the wall, just below the slopes of the roof, there was a space. And in this space, behind the owl, Solomon saw something move. He caught his breath. What was it? Could he really have been so lucky as to stumble on a nest?

He listened and watched. There was certainly one other owl, probably the female if it was a nest. But suppose there was more? Suppose there were eggs – or, even better, babies?

Solomon knew he ought not to look, that birds liked their nests kept secret. For several minutes he thought about it. Should he? Should he not? Probably it would be best to leave them alone – but when else might he get a chance to see a real owl's nest? Also, it might be dangerous: the beam creaked slightly every time he moved.

Curiosity got the better of him. Very carefully, bit by bit, he edged forward. He noticed a horrible smell, which got worse as he moved across: something between rotting meat and school toilets.

He was about half-way when the owl lowered his head and hissed loudly.

Solomon murmured, "It's all right. I won't hurt you. I—" The hissing had become a screech of unmistakable anger. The bird raised its wings as if to attack. Spread like that

it was huge and Solomon was afraid. He wobbled, but he was not going to turn back now. He glared back at the owl with equal determination.

Then something happened which made everything – even the danger he was in – worthwhile. From the space at the other end of the beam, two small faces peeped out and squeaked plaintively. They were magical: little balls of white fluff with round faces, as curious to see Solomon as he was to see them.

Suddenly Solomon heard the unmistakable sound of the beam he was on finally giving way. With screams of fear, first the father, then the mother owl flew up into the air and away.

Although Solomon moved back like lightning, he had not got far enough. With a rumble and a roar, the beam fell. Luckily for him, he landed on bales of hay. The air was thick with dust; he could feel it coating his face and the lashes of his closed eyes.

Something must have caught the side of his head; he put up his hand to feel blood mixing in with the grit and dust. But he wasn't hurt much. He lay there some moments, dizzy with relief.

On the ground the beam groaned and settled, though rubble still trickled down in dribs and drabs. Then silence.

Shaking the dust away Solomon got up and looked across. What of the baby owls? His stomach lurched. Where the nest had been was nothing: part of the wall had fallen with the beam.

He dared not look down. And when he did

it was every bit as bad as he feared.

Five metres below, the owl's nest lay in a mess of dirt and broken egg bits and yellow yolk. One owlet, perfect even in death, lay in the dirt, its head at an odd angle. Solomon turned away, and was quietly sick. Crouched on top of the hay bales he wept at his own stupidity, at the horror and waste of it all. It was all his own fault. Nothing could turn the clock back. Nothing could bring the baby owls back to life.

Chapter 6

Solomon climbed down very slowly. He picked up the baby owl and cradled it gently. It was still warm – almost hot – yet its head flopped with a horrible dead feeling. Solomon ached with guilt and sadness.

He buried it under a hedge. It was raining now, a dull drizzle. Josie turned up and watched with great interest. He had never been so close to a big dog before. He wished she'd go away. He put a large stone on top so she couldn't dig the owl up. Then he went back to find the other: he would bury them together.

Josie followed.

"Go away," he said nervously. Josie looked

at him steadily, but kept on. He couldn't tell if she were angry with him or not.

Coming back into the hayloft Solomon saw anew what a mess it was. He wondered how long it would be before Oakley found out. Probably he'd be sent straight back to the Home, and that would be an end to it all. Solomon didn't think he'd mind very much.

Now where was that other baby owl? Solomon looked under bits of wood and sifted through rubble. He felt Josie nose him on the leg and turned to see something dangling from her mouth. She had found it.

"Oh!" He was very much afraid of her. He thought in horror of her sharp teeth crunching the soft bones. "Give it here, Josie! Good dog," he said timidly, holding his hand out. Much to his surprise, Josie gave it to him.

Solomon took the little body. It was smaller than the other one, and didn't look nearly as nice. All the white fluff was mixed up with rubble dust and slobber from Josie's mouth and you could see the pink skin beneath, all criss-crossed with bluish veins. One of its legs looked crooked and there was blood on it.

Solomon shuddered. He was about to put it in his pocket in case Oakley appeared when he felt a strange throbbing in the palm of his hand. As he raised it in astonishment, he was sure he felt the tiny body move. Slowly, feebly, the little head turned from side to side. The owlet was not... quite... dead.

At that moment Solomon felt more horrified than pleased. What on earth should he do with a nearly dead chick? Of course he couldn't bury it now. Nor could he just put it down and leave it to die. One way or another he was stuck with it. It was very weak. But

suppose … just suppose it could live? He had to try.

He would ring Miss Bucket and tell her he didn't want to stay after all, and he'd keep the little bird hidden until he got back to the Home. That way, Oakley wouldn't know about the mess in the hayloft till after he'd gone.

The bird felt hot and heavy. Solomon looked it over carefully. One of its legs was certainly damaged, possibly broken. Suddenly Solomon was afraid: the responsibility was enormous.

He had no idea how to bring up a baby bird, let alone an injured one. Could he do it? And the more he thought, the more he realized he simply couldn't do it on his own. Gavin would just say it wasn't worth bothering about. He wouldn't help. The House Mother was always far too busy. The owl needed help at once. It might be too late if he waited till he got to the Home.

Solomon tucked it inside his jacket where it wouldn't be rained on. He headed towards the house with a feeling of dread.

Chapter 7

Solomon was not used to telling things to adults. This time he had to.

"What on earth have you done to yourself!" Oakley was shocked. The boy looked terrible. On the side of his head a lump was beginning to swell. Beneath the blood and dirt two lines of tears running down his cheeks showed how pale he was.

"Are you all right?"

"Yes, but—" Solomon took the baby owl from his pocket and held it out in cupped hands.

"What is it? Is it dead?"

"No," Solomon said.

Oakley found a bit of towel he used to dry

Josie on after a walk. Solomon put the baby owl down on it gently.

And as Oakley cleaned and dressed his cuts, Solomon told him everything. Oakley was furious. Solomon had nearly got himself killed – he'd been told not to go into the hayloft. Oakley dreaded Miss Birkett finding out. Was the boy going to be completely un-controllable? And what would Mr Locke say?

Solomon said, "Please – the owl. I'm fine now."

Oakley looked at it properly for the first time. The owlet was beginning to warm up a

bit. Its eyes were open, and it looked back at them fearfully. A feeble hiss came out of the curved pink beak.

"Can't we feed it milk or something? In a teaspoon?" Solomon suggested.

William Oakley shook his head. "Not milk. Not for a bird – I know that from Mr Locke's pheasants. They can't digest it properly. I'd get hold of our vet, but he's really more of a cow and horse man. I think he'd just suggest putting it out of its misery." He looked at Solomon. "You don't think … maybe we should—"

"Oh no!" Solomon was shocked.

"You see, owls and other raptors – birds of prey – are very different to anything our vet might come across. It might need special treatment. That leg needs attention."

"You mean that owls are like hawks and falcons and things?" He had suddenly remembered something. "That notice-board in my room. Wasn't there a place on that – a bird of prey place or something? It said 'falconry displays' and 'hawk preservation centre'. Would someone there know what to do?"

William Oakley jumped up. "Of course

they would! Quick, bring me the leaflet and I'll give them a ring."

Ten minutes later they were in a car, speeding through darkening lanes. Solomon looked into the box on his lap, where the sick bird lay beside a towel-wrapped bottle of hot water. The bird looked bedraggled and sad. It made no noise. Solomon talked to it quietly. William Oakley said nothing; just concentrated on getting there, fast.

" 'Through the twiddly gates'," Oakley said, slowing down. "These must be the ones he meant."

As they turned in, a woman came out of the gatehouse. She saw the box and smiled.

"Mr Oakley and Solomon – and a rescue? Murray Cluff – our vet – said you'd be along. Follow the signs to 'Falconry Displays', but turn in at the gate which says 'Private'. Bird Rescue's just in there."

Chapter 8

Murray Cluff had a thick puff of white hair and a face like a dried-up river bed, all criss-crossed with lines and lumpy. Solomon showed him the baby owl.

"Hmm," he growled. He looked at Solomon from under frosty eyebrows. "That looks like a broken leg to me. I'm not sure…" His large hands took up the little bird, holding it firmly but gently. "We'll need to X-ray to find out exactly. And there's a small graze on the end of its wing. That's no problem, I can clean it up and give you antibiotics for that. But if the leg is broken—" He paused. "We might have to put him down."

Solomon bit his lip and nodded.

The X-ray showed the leg was cracked –
just below the joint – but not broken.

"It's what we call a 'hairline' crack," Mr
Cluff said. "Almost a break, but not quite. At
his age the bones are quite soft – that's why it
looks odd."

Solomon's dark eyes were large. "Can you
mend it?"

"I'll try."

Solomon heaved a sigh of relief.

"Don't get too excited," Mr Cluff said.
"I'm warning you … he's very young, very
weak, and he's had a nasty shock. The chance
of him surviving is small.

"As he's so young I won't use a splint. I'll
fix the leg in place with tape. It'll need to stay
on for a couple of weeks while it heals. Then
– if he survives – you'll have to bring him
back to have it taken off.

"I'd let you leave him here, but we're up to
our necks already – a peregrine chick, three
Brahminny kites and a young tawny owl that
got knocked down by a car." He pointed to a
row of incubators on a bench.

"It'll be a lot of work – and most likely it'll

die anyway."

"I don't mind the work," Solomon looked at him anxiously. "I've got to try." He hesitated, touching the lump on his head. "You see – it – it was my fault."

The frosty brows shot up. "I see. Well, let's do something about this leg," Cluff said. "I'll do what I can. You wait here. I'll be a little while."

They waited. The room was small and stuffy. Solomon went over and peered into the incubators. The kites and peregrine were asleep, but the tawny owl blinked golden eyes at him. They all looked much stronger than his little owl.

Ten minutes later Cluff came back carrying another incubator. Flopped in the middle was the baby owl. It looked pathetic and ugly, its too-large head rolling lifelessly. Solomon looked at Cluff anxiously. His heart lurched. "Is he…?"

"He's not too bad. A bit groggy from the anaesthetic. We usually put birds under general anaesthetic – it lessens the shock of being handled. He can stay in this incubator till you go. I can't let you have it, in case I need it. I'll give you some food to take, though."

"How do I feed him?"

"I'll show you," Mr Cluff said. "Your little chap won't feel like eating yet. You can try with the peregrine – he's due for a feed."

An ancient fridge hummed in a corner. Cluff smiled. "This is the bit you won't like: getting the food ready. I'm afraid you'll need to develop a strong stomach."

"What is it?" Solomon asked.

"Mostly we use day-old chicks." Solomon winced.

"We can get hold of pheasant chicks at home," William Oakley said. "My boss keeps pheasants and there are always a few dead ones in the hatchery. And I've got a neighbour with a cat that keeps bringing in mice. She'd be glad if I sent Solomon in to take them off her."

"They'd do beautifully," said Cluff. "Even better as they're smaller."

Solomon couldn't stop himself from making a face. He guessed what was coming next...

"You have to chop them up, of course — bones, feathers and all. But that's what they need. Good roughage — like the muesli you have for breakfast."

"I don't think I'll ever be able to look at my breakfast again without thinking about this," Oakley said.

Murray Cluff took a bowl from the fridge and flipped open a porthole on the peregrine's incubator.

"This is Griff. We'll see if he can eat something to show you." He picked up some meat in a pair of tweezers.

William Oakley was surprised. "That's a huge lump. Won't he choke?"

"You wait," Cluff said. "It's amazing what they can stuff down. In the wild they'd be managing whole mice by the time they were three weeks old." He gently brushed the meat across the chick's beak. "Come on, Griff, do your stuff, eat up."

As if by magic, Griff's beak opened and he was able to pop the meat in. He pushed it in quite far.

"See — no problems swallowing. This is

what the mother bird does – brushes the beak like that. There are tiny, sensitive bristles on the side of the beak, and when these are touched – opening up is a natural reflex. Now you, Solomon. See if you can get it right … wait till he's finished that bit. Now."

Solomon did as he was told. He wasn't quite as good at it as Mr Cluff. He was too afraid of hurting the chick, and dropped the meat before it was properly inside.

"You'll learn and – if it decides to live – so will your owl."

He showed Solomon the amount to give each time. "Never, never overfeed. It's all too easily done when the bird just keeps opening its mouth for more. Owls can't be sick. They don't have a crop like other birds. The food just rots inside them – they get enteritis and die. And four times a day should be enough."

"But it's an owl. Won't it be asleep during the day?" Solomon asked.

"I'd like you to feed him first thing tomorrow as he's missed out today. After that he can fit in with you – barn owls are very good at adapting to a human timetable.

"Now then —" Murray Cluff shut the incubator and settled himself into an armchair — "I want to hear all about how your little owl got into this mess. Your fault, was it?"

Solomon told him everything. Cluff shook his head in despair.

"I suppose you know what you did was incredibly stupid? I'm not talking about you — if you want to go and kill yourself that's your lookout. I'm thinking about the owls. We need to look after every single wild barn owl we can."

Murray Cluff leant forward. The look he fixed on Solomon was laser sharp. Solomon shrank under it.

"We used to have thirty thousand wild pairs in Britain. Now we only have about three thousand."

"Only three thousand! Is that all?" Oakley said.

And I've cut that by several more, Solomon thought with shame.

"There are five times more tame barn owls than wild ones now," Murray Cluff told them.

Solomon was more determined than ever to make sure the owl lived. He imagined the moment of letting it go … the white wings soaring into midnight black. He swore to himself that his owl would have freedom. His owl would have chicks of its own one day.

"Did you know it was against the law to even go near its nest?"

Solomon shook his head.

"I wish more people did." Cluff spoke bitterly.

William Oakley was surprised. "Against the law? Just to go near an owl's nest?"

"Yes, and not only barn owls. Every hawk and falcon in this country is protected by the same law. Most will desert a nest if they think anyone knows about it. We've been so worried about barn owls that new laws were made to help them."

"Why did it happen? Why are there so few now?" Solomon asked.

"Lots of reasons, mostly to do with the way farming has changed recently. Owls hunt in long grass along the edges of fields. Most of our woods and hedgerows have gone and those were the main hunting grounds for barn owls. Weedkillers and insecticides don't help – there's nothing for mice to eat in a nice clean field of silage grass. So the mice went…"

"And the owls went with them," said Oakley.

"It's a pretty gloomy picture," Cluff said. "But let's see if we can manage to keep this one."

He went out, coming back a moment later with a large cardboard box, which he plonked on the table. "I'll give you this and you can borrow a heat lamp: you'll need that for the first day or so."

The vet ferreted around in a cupboard and came out with a big lamp on the end of a long flex, and a roll of toilet paper. As they watched, he made a hole in one end of the box, wiggled the lamp into place and fixed it with masking tape.

"The lamp must be in the right place – not so high that it doesn't keep him warm enough, but not so low that it could burn him. And you need a box this size so he can move away if he gets too hot."

He tore off a strip of toilet roll and scrumpled it up, then flung the roll at Solomon. "You do some, too – this is his nest."

Solomon scrumpled away, throwing lumps of tissue in the box until there was a nice, warm layer.

"Wouldn't straw be better?" asked Oakley.

"Tissue is much more absorbent. If you're looking after a sick bird, you want to keep it very clean – as much for your own sake as the owl's. Owl's nests are very nasty places indeed – a real mess of pellets and rotting food."

"Oh yes," remembered Solomon. "It did smell horrible."

Murray Cluff switched on the lamp. "That's done." He fetched the little owl and put it in the box. It raised its head, huge on the little thin neck, then dropped it again feebly.

Cluff shook his head. "It's not strong," he said.

Oakley watched Solomon: the sharp face looking so serious now, the black hair. He wasn't the fair, solid child Oakley had always imagined he and Sonia would have. That child would not have disobeyed him so easily, would never have done something so wild and crazy.

Solomon yawned, and Oakley looked at his watch. Past one o'clock in the morning – and they still had to get back!

As they drove off, Murray Cluff gave them a warning. "Don't give it a name till you know it has survived – say three nights. Ring any time to tell me how you are getting on."

In its box, the little owl grumbled in its sleep.

Chapter 9

Solomon raced down to the kitchen. With curtains drawn it was still dark; the clock in the hall read six minutes past five. He heard Josie creak to her feet. He could just about see her yawn and stretch in the light from the box in the corner. There was no sound coming from it, and he looked in with beating heart.

The owlet lay huddled in a corner, quite still. Solomon held his breath, getting himself ready for disappointment. But once he looked more carefully he could see a fluttering pulse: the owl was breathing.

"It's alive!" he told Josie. Josie wagged her tail, pleased at being spoken to so early in the morning. Solomon wasn't afraid of Josie now. He was learning to tickle her behind the ears in the way she liked best.

A hoarse complaining noise came from the box. Solomon was delighted. "That means it's hungry," he told Josie, tickling her behind the ears. "And that's a good sign." Josie grunted with pleasure.

The noise came again. Solomon rushed off to the fridge. He shuddered, then screwed up his courage. He found a jam-jar and put the right number of chopped lumps in it. He

mixed in the medicine, trying not to look too closely.

This time the owl was looking up. It was still very weak, but all the down had fluffed out. It didn't look much like an owl yet – more like a baby vulture in a powder puff. The black eyes blinked at him, surprised.

Solomon tapped it on the beak the way Mr Cluff had shown him. At first nothing happened. Perhaps the little bird was too frightened – or had he done it wrong? But then it opened up and Solomon was able to poke in a scrap of meat. The second time, he couldn't get it to open its beak at all. Perhaps it didn't like the taste of medicine?

Its eyes closed, and whenever Solomon tried, it just shook its head crossly and went back to sleep.

"Please, owl," Solomon pleaded. He couldn't force it. What should he do? He decided to wait ten minutes and try again.

And this time the little owl fed. Not all at once – it was still too weak. But bit by bit, scrap by scrap, Solomon fed it until it could take no more.

When William Oakley came down much later, everything was quiet. The baby owl was in his box, fast asleep. Solomon had somehow managed to crawl into Josie's basket, and they too slept in a warm tangle of boy and dog.

But all that first day, and the next, things were difficult. Every time Solomon tried to feed it the same thing happened: the owl cried, but then turned away. Sometimes Solomon felt like crying with frustration. Sometimes he almost gave up. He hated how it shook with fear whenever he came near, but was too weak to cry out properly or move away. It seemed almost mean to carry on.

But Solomon did carry on. Every feed took ages – but in the end, he always got the food into it.

"You're not out of the woods yet," warned Murray Cluff, who phoned to see how they were getting on. "Sometimes everything seems to be swimming along, then – wham! – it decides it doesn't like being fed by humans, or a sudden noise shocks it – all your work's wasted and it's lying there like an old dish-mop, doggo, dead as a doornail."

Miss Birkett phoned too. "So that's why you wanted to know about owls, is it? I am glad that it's all working out," she said with relief in her voice.

Chapter 10

Towards the end of the third day, the owl seemed a bit better. By the last feed there was a real improvement. When Solomon appeared with his tweezers and nasty lump of meat, the little owl hissed loudly and opened his beak before Solomon had even got near. This time it ate all the food eagerly. It was looking a bit more perky too: the medicine was beginning to do its job.

"Looks as though you've done it. What are you calling it, then?" Solomon could almost see Murray Cluff's pleased grin down the phone.

Solomon had been thinking about this. "Barney," he said.

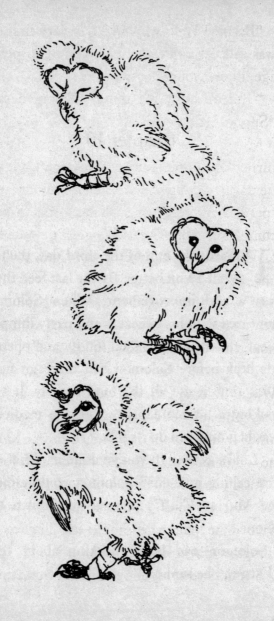

"Barney! Well, why not? My very first owl was called Barney, too. He lived to a ripe old age. I hope yours does, too."

"There's only one thing," Solomon said. "Suppose it's a girl?"

Murray Cluff laughed. "...as my Barney turned out to be. You certainly can't tell yet. Females are usually a richer colour with speckles on the front. Males often have a completely white breast. You can't always tell ... one way or another you've got a 50–50 chance. How's the leg?"

"Fine," Solomon said. "He can't stand up very well. But mostly he hardly seems to notice it. And the wing's healed fine."

When Solomon wasn't feeding Barney or changing his bedding – or all the thousand other things Solomon found to do for him – he wandered the fields and woods with Josie.

Josie was a brilliant companion. She didn't tell him not to do things as an adult would have done (and she didn't tell him to do things as Gavin Bratley had).

She noticed everything, though. Sometimes

she went suddenly still, ears pricked, nose sniffing. If Solomon looked the way her nose pointed there was always something there – usually a rabbit feeding, once a speckled brown pheasant with a family of ten chicks.

And she did care about him. Once, down by the river, Solomon felt like a swim. He took all his clothes off and left them in a pile. Solomon sucked his breath in sharply as his foot touched water. It was much colder than a swimming pool – but that made it exciting. Mud squished up between his toes, and there were sharp things in it.

With a yelp, Solomon leapt right in. And Josie went frantic. Josie wasn't a barking sort of dog usually. Now she barked, ran towards the cottage, then back to Solomon. Back and forth she went, barking all the time. Any moment, she would run off and fetch William Oakley.

As quickly as he could, Solomon got out and dressed: but it was a struggle. The watery tug on his limbs had frightened him. He knew Josie was right, and he never did it again.

Miss Birkett phoned every evening. She was delighted when he asked if he could stay

on longer. "Of course you can. I've spoken to my area supervisor, and though you'll be missing more school, we all feel this is much more important. It's almost end of term, anyway. If everything goes well, you can start locally next term."

Missing a bit of school didn't bother Solomon one bit. But the missing Sonia did. She was still away. Solomon had a feeling Miss Birkett would take him back at once if she knew about that. At the moment, all Solomon could think about was Barney. So he just said 'fine' to whatever Miss Birkett asked.

When she asked about Sonia, he changed the subject so carefully she didn't notice. But on the walks with Josie he thought about Sonia a lot. He didn't really think William Oakley could have murdered her now. So where was she?

Chapter 11

Barney grew stronger. He turned from a weak and frightened creature into a very lively snowball.

Like any wild bird, he was nervous of humans, and if Solomon's head appeared rather suddenly over the edge of the box, he would "play dead" by falling over backwards with his eyes closed. The first time it happened, Solomon thought something terrible had happened. But Barney was a pretty useless actor, because after a few seconds he looked round to see if Solomon was still there.

Murray Cluff laughed when Solomon told him. "I've been caught out myself by that one

– all barn owls do it. They're cunning though. You wait till he's a bit bigger: he may be on his back, but the little beggar will make sure he's got his claws facing you – and he'll use them! Barn owls have got claws like needles."

Solomon watched Barney for hours. Though he tried not to make any sudden moves, he noticed the owl was getting more used to him. He loved picking Barney up and holding him. The white down was wonderfully soft, and there was more of it every day.

At first he wondered why. Then he worked it out: as wild owls grow, the mother bird has to spend more and more time out of the nest getting them food. The owlets huddle together in an owly duvet to keep warm.

Solomon's favourite thing about Barney was when he bounced his head around as if he were dancing to fast rock music. It looked completely daft, for however fast his head moved – up and down or side to side – his face stayed flat, as if it were on rails. Sometimes he flapped his stumpy wings at the same time. Solomon collapsed laughing.

Mr Cluff said it was all just getting his muscles exercised, but Solomon was convinced otherwise: "You said his hearing was millions of times better than ours. I bet there's a car passing – miles away somewhere – and he's listening to the radio."

But things didn't always go smoothly. One day Barney went missing.

"William!" Startled, Oakley came in from the garden: it was the first time Solomon had called him by his name – usually he avoided it, or said "Mr Oakley". He knew it must be something serious.

"Barney's gone!"

"He can't have," Oakley said. But Barney's box was empty.

Solomon had just moved the box away from the corner. Barney no longer needed the heat lamp and Solomon couldn't see in unless it was in better light. The box was higher and Solomon had to stand on a chair to get to it.

"If he jumped out he might have hurt himself," Solomon said worriedly. They scrabbled around under the chair.

Oakley said, "He can't have jumped out – not with his leg in a bandage."

And Barney's wings were just little fluffy stumps – he couldn't have flown away. They searched the room, and then the house from top to bottom.

It just didn't seem possible that he could have disappeared. Yet he had. Solomon tried to be calm. It was no use giving up.

"We should stand and listen; he's always making that hissing noise…" William Oakley said. They listened, but all they could hear was Josie's heavy breathing and her claws on the tiled floor. She thrust her nose into Oakley's hand, and wagged her tail at him.

Solomon remembered something. "Josie found Barney in the beginning. Maybe she can find him now?" he said.

"Mmm." Oakley wasn't sure he wanted Josie to find Barney before he did: that silence was worrying. Could the cat from next door have come in and…? But Solomon was already off.

"Come on, Josie – find – good dog – find Barney."

Josie wagged her tail harder, but didn't move.

"Please," Solomon said. "You try," he said to Oakley.

Oakley did, but Josie just sat. She hung her head and whined. "Come on, Josie," Oakley said more firmly. "Find Barney."

And this time Josie went. They followed close behind, encouraging her with cries of "Good dog!" and "Good girl, Josie!"

She led them out of the back door, and across the yard, head held low.

"She's smelling him!" Solomon cried, full of hope.

"That's funny," Oakley said. "I know the hayloft door was only open a crack this morning. Have you been in again, Solomon? I hope—"

Solomon shook his head. "No."

Oakley was getting to know Solomon. He knew Solomon was telling the truth.

"OK. I'll go first," he said. The hayloft had been cleaned up since the awful day of the accident, but the broken beam still lay on one side. Solomon's heart beat a twinge of fear and guilt at the reminder. He was startled out of this by a small hiss.

"Barney!" They both saw him at the same time: very much alive, and very cross. Solomon rushed to pick him up. He checked him all over, but Barney seemed to be completely unharmed. Solomon rubbed his beak and the hiss turned to a little rippling squeak of pleasure.

"How did he get there?" he wondered.

It was William Oakley who first realized what had happened.

"Josie!" he said sternly. "You're a bad dog. Come back here!"

And Josie, who was trying to sneak away, wagged her tail hard, and hung her head in guilt.

William Oakley told her off severely. "She must have jumped up on the chair. She could reach him from there. We must be quite sure she doesn't do it again – next time he might really be hurt."

"I'll move the chair away each time," Solomon said. "I didn't think about Josie. But why did she do it?"

Oakley thought a bit. "I wonder … maybe she's jealous of all the attention Barney's been getting."

"Poor Josie," Solomon said.

Chapter 12

"It must be time to take Barney's tape off," Murray Cluff said.

"He's grown so much," Solomon said. "It does look a bit tight."

"Would you and your dad have time to bring him round this afternoon? I'll show you both round. I need to talk to you about something… Hello? Are you still there?"

"Yes," Solomon managed. His "dad"! He and Oakley looked so different but Cluff had not even questioned it. He felt so peculiar he forgot to wonder what it was Cluff thought so important. And he'd been so interested in Barney he'd pushed aside the whole reason why he was at Screech Cottage in the first place.

"Good. See you then." Cluff rang off.

In the afternoon, Solomon fed Barney a very small extra feed in case he was upset by the journey and didn't want anything later. And Barney got furious. He opened his eyes wide, bounced his head up and down and made snoring noises at Solomon. "Hey! What's this? More food! More food! Where's the rest of it, eh?"

Solomon shut him in a box to the sound of loud snores, which got louder and angrier as Barney realized he wasn't going to get more. Solomon was looking forward to showing Cluff how well Barney was. He had just packed the box in the car (Barney still protesting noisily) when the phone rang.

Solomon ran back. "I'll get it."

Solomon wasn't thinking about Miss Birkett, and he hadn't prepared what to say. This time she asked him outright about Sonia, and he couldn't avoid giving the truth away.

"I see," said Miss Birkett thoughtfully. "Is Mr Oakley there?"

Solomon wanted to be off. He could see

William Oakley opening the gate to let the car out.

"Er … no." It was sort of true.

"Sorry – got to go," he said, and put the phone down.

"You're doing a good job." Solomon scooped Barney up, so Murray Cluff could examine him properly. "He's growing well… Hey! watch it with those claws."

Barney hissed loudly, and lashed out with his good leg. Murray Cluff yelled, "Ouch! Wretched bird. I should have put gloves on."

Solomon tried not to look smug – Barney was never that fierce with him any more. Murray Cluff carefully unwound the tape, and checked the leg.

"He seems surprisingly well." Cluff's face scrumpled into a river-bed smile. He stood Barney down.

Barney swivelled his head round and examined Cluff from the other way up. Then he turned his back on them and bobbed his head up and down, sneaking cross looks at them now and then.

But when Barney discovered his leg wasn't stiff and heavy any more, he cheered up. First he hopped forward. Then he bent down to look at his leg from all angles.

"Haagh?" he said in a surprised way. And "Haagh!" again.

Then he hopped all round the table, faster and faster – Murray Cluff caught him just in time.

"You're not ready for flying yet, young chap."

Barney screeched like mad at being caught, and flapped his stumpy wings frantically. Cluff popped him back in his box.

"Come and see round. I want to show you something," the vet said.

Chapter 13

"We don't just have falcons and hawks here – our owls are very popular with everyone. We've got birds of prey from all over the world."

They were walking down a grassy avenue. On either side of them were cages so large that small trees grew in them quite freely. You had to search hard amongst the leaves to find the birds that lived there.

"I didn't know there were so many different owls – I like those great big stripey ones," Oakley said.

"Those are wood owls, from Kenya. How about these burrowing ones?"

One popped up just as they passed, and

Solomon smiled: he liked the burrowing owls very much.

"And this is our British Isles section. Short-eared owls first – can you see the chicks?"

Solomon nodded. Four fluffy grey owls sat in different parts of the aviary. All but one were fast asleep. "They look more like that baby tawny you had."

"Right," said Mr Cluff. "That's just what they are. We always use foster parents if we're returning birds to the wild."

Solomon had no time to think about this, for Murray Cluff was moving on.

"Come and see Freda the barn owl... Here, take this glove, you'll need it."

A moment later, Solomon was holding a fully grown, live barn owl. He kept his hand very still, holding his breath so as not to disturb her. Freda looked at him with interest, blinking her black eyes at him. She was beautiful.

Solomon stroked her gently. "Her feathers are as soft as Barney's down." She looked big, but she was lighter than he'd expected.

"Owls are much smaller than you think –

they're mostly feathers. It's all because of the way they hunt. Hawks and falcons use speed to catch their food. But owls are slow, precision hunters. When all the others are tucked up in their nests, they sit around in the cold night air. They wait. And watch. And listen. A deep layer of feathers keeps them both warm — and quiet. Barn owls are absolutely silent when they fly."

"She's wonderful," Solomon said. And yet — yet something bothered him.

"Very tame, isn't she?" Oakley said.

That was it! Tame — that was what was

wrong. Solomon said, "I want Barney to be free. Why don't you set Freda free?"

"She is… Hold your hand up … off you go, Freda!"

Solomon held his hand up and Freda soared into the air, turned a few circles and landed on a fence post some way off.

"She's in perfect condition. She could fly off if she wanted to. But she won't. She was brought in as a chick like Barney, and reared by us – like Barney. It would have been very hard to put her back into the wild."

"Barney's different, though. Barney's

going back to the wild." Solomon was very sure of this. If there were so few wild barn owls left – he just had to. "You said 'hard' – not impossible. I don't mind hard things."

"For Barney, Solomon, I'm afraid it is impossible. You see—"

Solomon remembered the moments after his fall: the smashed eggs, the dead chick, the parent birds flying – as he guessed – as far away as they could from their destroyed family.

"No! It can't be. What about fostering? Like those ones you showed me? Haven't you got another one who could foster Barney?"

"Those tawny chicks weren't injured. We didn't handle them right from the start."

"But—"

"Listen," Cluff said. "You can't release Barney into the wild. First, you need a 'scientific licence' from the government. And it's very hard indeed to get one."

"I'll do it – I'll get one," Solomon said.

Murray Cluff looked into Solomon's determined face and spoke quietly, but firmly. "Not, I'm afraid, for Barney. For a start, it takes over a year. You have to write a log-book. Interview people. Be inspected – and there's lots more."

"A year!" Solomon couldn't believe it. "But I want Barney to go back to the wild. I want him to grow up and have chicks of his own. So what I did is made right."

Murray Cluff tried to be kind. But there was no getting away from the truth.

"It would be cruel to release Barney into the wild. That's why there are such strict laws against it. Barney might learn to catch the odd mouse – Freda does sometimes – but he'd never catch enough to live on. He'd die.

"Owls learn from their parents – and you are Barney's parent, as far as he can see. People always think that if they let their tame owl free it will learn to live naturally. It won't. Almost certainly it will die a slow and cruel death from starvation."

Murray Cluff continued: "I got you here today for a reason. Firstly to say what I have just said. But there's something else. Even if you can't let Barney go, there's a lot you can do. Think about Barney's parents. You destroyed their chances of bringing up that brood of chicks. But what's happened to them?"

Solomon bit his lip and looked at the ground. Murray Cluff certainly didn't believe in soft words. Solomon wriggled uncomfortably.

"This is how you can help. Owls like nesting in the same place year after year. However, from what you say, their home would have been destroyed in a few months anyway."

Solomon nodded.

"Barn conversions have been yet another nail in the barn owls' coffin. Especially when there's nowhere else for them to go. I'd like you to put up a nesting box nearby – preferably several so they can choose."

"You mean they might not have flown away after all?"

"They'll be roosting somewhere near."

"Then they might have more chicks? Soon? Won't they be too upset?"

"They might be. Tawny owls wouldn't be – barn owls are much more sensitive."

Solomon was thinking: I can't set Barney

free, but if I can get the owls to nest again, that will make up for what I did. He was disappointed in one way, but then – he could keep Barney. For ever! It meant he must stay at Screech Cottage. To be adopted by William and … and Sonia? Did he want that? If only Sonia would come back!

"What about food?" Solomon asked. "When the barn is converted all the mice will go."

William Oakley groaned. "Into our house, I expect."

Murray Cluff laughed. "I expect Mrs Oakley won't be too pleased about that." Solomon looked quickly at Oakley, but Oakley avoided his eye. It was more obvious than ever that Oakley was hiding something from him. There was some mystery about Sonia.

It wasn't long before he found out.

Chapter 14

Driving back, Solomon kept looking at Oakley. He'd always thought he'd have a father who was dark and very handsome. He'd be full of interesting talk and immediately say the sort of things to make Solomon feel at home. Oakley was none of these things – more red and stubby, and rather awkward.

Oakley didn't notice Solomon's gaze. His face was set in thought. Josie sat in the back with her grey muzzle on his shoulder.

"She misses Sonia," Oakley said without thinking.

Solomon caught his breath: it was now or never. He said, "When is Sonia coming? Why isn't she here?"

He wasn't prepared for the answer. William Oakley didn't say anything for a minute. When he did the words came out slowly, like squeezing a tube of dried-up toothpaste.

"I should have told you before. Only I couldn't believe it myself."

Solomon wondered what was coming next.

"She isn't coming back."

"But why? Where is she?"

"She – she's left me. For someone else."

It had all come to a head a few days before Solomon arrived. Oakley thought that Sonia leaving meant the adoption was off – that's why he was so surprised when Solomon turned up after all.

"Oh." It was all Solomon could say. So there was going to be no mother. No real family after all. Nothing. A dull feeling twisted in Solomon's stomach. He swallowed hard.

Oakley carried on. "We always wanted children. And – I – I've got something wrong with me. I couldn't. We've been waiting and waiting to adopt. She'd been a bit funny for some time, but I thought we'd be fine once we had you.

"Now she wants to marry this other bloke. She's going to have his baby." William Oakley tried to grin. "I suppose you just came too late for Sonia."

Solomon felt sorry for him. Wanting a child and not being able to have one wasn't that different from wanting parents and not being able to have them. He thought: at least I know now. And it makes it easier. I don't want to stay if there's no mother, and Oakley won't want me to.

Then he felt angry with Oakley. It just wasn't fair! He needn't have lied, after all. Solomon would have gone straight back to the Home. He'd never have gone up into the hayloft and Barney would never have fallen and – oh, Barney! What about Barney? If Barney couldn't go back to the wild what would happen to him?

In just a short time, so much had happened. He couldn't take Barney back with him – not to a city, not to the Home. He couldn't expect William Oakley to look after him.

Solomon forced his voice to sound calm. "When Barney's grown, I'm sure Mr Cluff would take him. Freda's quite old now. I know he'll want another tame barn owl, because she's so popular with the visitors. Can I stay till he goes? A few more weeks?"

"Stay?" William Oakley shot an odd look at him. "Yes. Yes, you can."

Anger took over again. "Why didn't you tell me!" Solomon almost spat it out. He turned away and kept his face pressed against the window for the rest of the journey.

Chapter 15

Solomon went up to his bedroom, and curled up on the bed. Outside it was getting dark. He knew it was past supper, but he didn't feel hungry. His mind was in a tangle. He'd sort of known all along – but he'd just kept hoping Sonia would turn up. Now it was certain. He wasn't going to have a mother after all.

Solomon felt angry and cheated. He hated William Oakley for not telling him before. More than anything he hated Sonia. Disappointment cut into him like a knife.

He sneaked down and fetched Josie. She felt warm and comforting, though she did smell a bit. He hoped William Oakley wouldn't notice the muddy pawmarks and hairs all over the bedclothes. Too bad if he did. Josie heaved a deep sigh of pleasure, rested her grey nose on his chest, and went to sleep. He would miss her, too, when he went.

Out of the silence came a long, trembling cry. An owl! The owls were back. Almost before poor Josie had wakened, Solomon darted to the window and peered out. He couldn't see it, but it was there all right.

He raced down to tell Oakley. "They're back!" he cried. "Barney's parents! Come and

listen! They haven't gone after all."

A mutter of voices from the sitting room told him Oakley probably hadn't heard: they had a visitor. Suppose Sonia had changed her mind? Was it her? Solomon hesitated, then turned the handle. William Oakley jumped up. He looked even more red and uncomfortable than usual.

"Hello, Solomon," said Miss Birkett.

Solomon scowled at her.

Miss Birkett wore a very serious face. Today the lipstick was mostly in the right place, and was the colour of a plastic doll. Solomon wanted to tell her it made him feel sick.

"Mr Oakley's been telling me. About why Mrs Oakley isn't here."

Solomon nodded. "Yes."

Miss Birkett sighed. "Oh dear – and I had thought you were beginning to get on so well. This changes everything."

Of course it changes everything, you stupid Bucket, thought Solomon. I won't have a mother!

William Oakley mumbled, "I – I'm sorry." He added guiltily, "Er, Solomon, you haven't had anything to eat yet."

Solomon was prickling with anger. He fiddled with a light switch. He saw it was annoying them, so he did it again. He did it fourteen times to make them really riled.

"It's all right. I'm not hungry… Well, not very," he said at last.

Solomon imagined the report Miss Birkett would be writing: "Mr Oakley lied about why his wife was not at home. He also forgot to feed the boy."

William Oakley looked guiltier than ever, and Solomon began to feel less angry. Perhaps he'd punished him enough.

"You realize that this means you will be going back to the Home?"

Solomon nodded.

"What about your baby owl, Solomon?" Miss Birkett said.

Solomon told her about Mr Cluff. "At the moment Barney needs a lot of looking after, and Mr Cluff's always busy. But I'm pretty sure he'll take Barney when he's grown – when he can fly. He's growing fast. I just want to stay till he goes. It won't be long."

Miss Birkett turned to Oakley.

"That's fine," Oakley said.

There goes the lipstick again! thought Solomon, for Miss Birkett's hand had gone to her mouth again. She frowned. "How long will you need?"

Solomon hesitated: he didn't want to get in William Oakley's way – but he had to be sure Barney was all right. "Six weeks?"

"I'll need to check with the Area Supervisor. I'll see what I can do."

A lot happened in that six weeks: some of it good, some of it so awful that nothing else mattered at all.

Chapter 16

For the first couple of weeks things went on much as usual. Barney was growing fast. He was much too large for his box now. William Oakley built him a large aviary outside. One warm afternoon they put him in it for a few hours. They put the box on its side so he could get out when he wanted.

Solomon watched. At first Barney just sat in a corner. Every now and then he hissed quietly, unhappily. After a bit he bobbed his head round the corner and looked out, snatching it in again quickly. More hissing. More bobbing. It was half an hour and many sneaky looks later before he dared venture out of the box.

After that, Barney went out for a while every day. Under the white fluff, his wings were getting longer. He liked to stretch them out, testing the new pinion feathers in the air. Soon he could stay in the aviary most of the time.

Sometimes Josie lay down beside Solomon and watched too, though Barney bobbed his head at her and hissed at her fiercely.

Solomon noticed she wasn't so keen to go on walks with him. Did she know he wasn't staying? Or was it just her old jealousy of Barney? Was she annoyed? He was a bit hurt.

*　*　*

"Look what I've got, Barney," Solomon said. "A fieldmouse the neighbour's cat brought in." So far he'd given Barney chopped meat. He wondered if Barney could swallow the mouse whole.

Barney put his head on one side and made his snory begging call. When Solomon hesitated he waddled up and grabbed it himself.

It was a bit of a struggle. Barney's eyes bulged. Solomon swore he could see them watering. He tried to take it away – suppose Barney choked? But Barney wouldn't let him. He turned his back on Solomon and hopped to the other end of his box, making the most revolting, greedy gulping noise. At last he got it down.

"You're gross," Solomon told him in disgust. Barney blinked at him sleepily and belched out a large pellet.

Whenever he spent too long watching Barney, Josie always came over and nudged him on the leg with her nose. "Don't be so jealous," he told her.

* * *

Solomon would remember that evening for a long time. Oakley had been working hard. He came in and said: "I'm shattered. There's no food in the house, and I'm starving... Let's eat out."

Solomon had never been to a restaurant before. The place smelled of good cooking and freshly pressed linen. In the corner, a huge trolley was stacked with the sort of puddings Solomon had only dreamed about – great lumps of chocolatey fudgey stuff, strawberry tarts dizzy with cream. Oakley chose a steak, and suggested Solomon have the pizza, "...and the trolley after?"

Oakley had a glass of red wine, and gave Solomon a little sip. Solomon screwed up his face. "It's sour!" He wondered how anyone could like wine.

The waitress had shining fair hair, tied back in a floaty blue scarf, and a very tight, very short skirt. Her lipstick didn't run in a smudge down her face. Solomon was afraid of speaking to someone so glamorous at first, but by the end of the meal they were calling her Jackie, and chatting and making jokes with her. And she sneaked extra chocolates for Solomon with William Oakley's coffee.

It was a wonderful evening. Josie was curled up in her basket when they got back. She looked gloomy.

"She's sulking," Oakley said. "All the attention on Barney, and then us abandoning her for the evening. Poor old Josie."

Solomon made a fuss of her, and she gave a creaky sigh, and licked him gratefully. It's funny, I was so afraid of her at first, he thought.

Chapter 17

Six weeks, five weeks, four – they seemed to roll by. Almost every morning Solomon was up before Oakley; he liked being the first to greet Josie – she was always so pleased to see him – then he would let Barney out of his box.

He liked to sit and have a quiet breakfast on his own, with Barney hopping about the kitchen, or jumping on his shoulder and rubbing his ear with his beak. When Barney did this, Josie always stumped over and put her head on his knee. "Jealous old thing," he would say, and rub her behind the ears till she grunted with pleasure.

But one morning Josie didn't bother to get

up. "What's the matter? Cross with me again?" Solomon asked. But Josie wasn't cross. She kept her nose on her paws and watched him with her large brown eyes as he got his cereal and ate it slowly.

Halfway through the morning, Oakley came in for coffee.

"I don't think Josie's well," Solomon said.

"P'raps she's just feeling a bit arthritic." Oakley stooped to pat her head. "She's getting on now. I expect she's starting to feel her age."

Josie stayed in her basket most of the morning. She got up when Solomon put out her lunch, but she didn't eat much: Josie usually guzzled everything you gave her. Solomon had learned not to leave the butter on the table – it was always gone when he came back.

Perhaps a special treat was called for. He put a dab of butter on his finger and offered it to her: Josie licked it up politely, but he could see she didn't really want it.

That evening things suddenly got worse.

"It's Josie," Solomon said. There was a

sharp edge to his voice that made Oakley drop what he was doing and run.

William Oakley took one look at her. "I'll call the vet," he said.

Dogs can't sweat; instead they pant. Josie's flanks heaved as if from a long, hard run. Her eyes watched them anxiously. She was very hot.

Solomon held out a bowl of water. She lapped up a little, and thumped her tail gratefully.

"She'll be all right, won't she?" Solomon asked. William Oakley stroked the dog's head gently. "I wish the vet would come."

The vet came. "I'll give her a shot to make her more comfortable. And I'll leave you some medicine." He hesitated. "She's had a good, long life. Call me in the morning if she gets worse."

What does he mean "had"? Solomon wondered. He's talking about her as if she were dead.

William Oakley insisted Solomon went to bed. But an hour later he came down with his duvet wrapped round him.

"I can't sleep."

"Nor can I. How about some hot chocolate?"

Solomon nodded. After the injection the vet had given her, Josie fell asleep. Her breathing became calmer, and she looked better.

Oakley put on a video to pass the time, and they watched it sleepily. Every now and then one of them got up to check on Josie, but she was sleeping peacefully. Towards midnight, she woke, and struggled to get up.

"I think she's better!" Solomon wriggled into her basket and sat with her grey head on

his lap. William Oakley sat on the floor next to him.

Josie yawned in a pleased sort of way and looked up at them comfortably. She seemed tired. Solomon stroked her. But quite suddenly, she began to pant again. Her soft eyes seemed anxious. One last time she reached out and nudged William, then Solomon, with her nose. A minute later it was all over.

William Oakley put his hand on Solomon's shoulder. He just gripped it gently. Then he said, "I think she's dead, isn't she?"

Solomon nodded. His thin shoulders began to shake. William Oakley kept his hand where it was. They stayed like that for a long time. Neither of them made a sound, but the air between them was damp with tears.

Chapter 18

It was strange that morning. Solomon felt raw as an onion with the thin skin peeled away. Probably William Oakley felt the same. Everything went on as usual – the sun shone as it always did, and there was a smell of hot grass from the compost heap – but it was a new world. A world without Josie.

And then Miss Birkett turned up. "This will be my last visit."

Solomon wished she'd hurry up and go.

"Only ten more days." She had arrived just as they were digging a grave for Josie. It was under the same hedge where Solomon had buried the baby owl, a little way along.

But Miss Birkett wouldn't go. She stayed

ages and ages — far longer than usual. She kept saying how sorry she was to hear about Josie, but she didn't seem to understand that they just wanted to be alone. In the end, Oakley asked her quite bluntly to leave.

They buried Josie in the blanket she always slept on. William Oakley carried her over, wrapped in it. Solomon took a last peek. She was too stiff to be asleep, but it was still Josie.

Barney was perched on Solomon's shoulder. Solomon said: "It's a complete opposite from when I buried Barney's brother. That time Josie watched him being buried. Now she's dead and he's watching her." He could hardly watch the first shower of earth cover the familiar shape.

When they had finished, Oakley rested on his spade, and they both stood in thought. Josie dying like that had stirred things up in Solomon. Sorted some out, muddied others. Barney bent down and nibbled Solomon's ear. Ten days! Solomon at last realized how short it was. In ten days he would be back with Gavin Bratley, the House Mother and everything at the Home. Was that really what he wanted?

"She was a good friend," Oakley said.

When Solomon spoke, it wasn't about Josie at all. In a very small voice, almost a whisper, he asked something he'd been wanting to know a long time.

"William, that first day I came. Why did you lie?"

Oakley blew his nose. He was embarrassed. "I suppose I shouldn't have. I got you into all this mess. No, I knew Sonia wouldn't come back really. I lied because ... I wanted you so much. Even if she didn't."

"Oh." Solomon hadn't thought of it that way round. Thoughts were all bumping round in his mind. "And now?"

Oakley wasn't very good at this sort of thing. It made him all hot and awkward. "Oh yes. Still do. A lot. Want you, I mean," he mumbled.

This time Solomon's voice was so small Oakley had to strain to hear it at all: "Me too," he said.

William Oakley said nothing for a few minutes. His heart was too full. He wanted to hug Solomon, but that would disturb Barney on his shoulder. After all, Barney was part of it all. He was another member of the family. Instead, Oakley put his hand out. "Shake?"

Solomon took the large red hand in his own and looked up at Oakley solemnly. Then Oakley smiled. It was the warmest, kindest, biggest smile anyone had ever given Solomon. Very seriously, he gave one back.

Chapter 19

It was an odd day — a sort of happy-sad day. William Oakley decided not to work. "Mr Locke will understand."

They kept looking at each other and remembering. He's going to be my father! Solomon kept thinking. I'm not going back to the Home. I'm going to belong to him, and he's going to belong to me.

He couldn't understand why it had taken him so long to realize. And every time he thought about it he couldn't help taking in a sharp breath of air and shooting a big smile at Oakley.

"It's a pity Josie didn't know," Oakley said. "She'd have been so pleased."

Of course Solomon was sorry not to have a mother as well as William. Sometimes things don't work out exactly the way you expect – but they can still be good. So Oakley wasn't dark and handsome? So what? He was good and kind and Solomon liked him very much indeed. That was the important thing.

Only one thing bothered him: "What about Miss Birkett? I mean, you did trick her – about Sonia."

"Oh, don't worry about her." William Oakley was far too happy to be reminded about that. "What I said won't matter when they know why I did it – because I wanted you so much. What could be better than wanting you?" He grinned. "We'll talk her round."

He and Solomon spent the rest of the day making a couple of nesting boxes for Barney's parents. They weren't difficult to make – Murray Cluff had told them how. Then they had to find the best places to put them up.

"Not facing south or they'll bake, Mr Cluff said – and quite sheltered so the chicks are safe when they start coming out of the nest."

Everything fitted together now; Solomon would be able to see if Barney's parents liked their new home. He would be there to see if they brought up another brood of chicks. He would do everything in his power to help.

William Oakley even said he would speak to Mr Locke about it. "I'll ask if we can leave a wider band of rough grass round all his fields for them to hunt along. I think he'd be keen to encourage wildlife – and everybody likes barn owls."

Best of all Solomon wouldn't have to give Barney back. Barney was looking rather strange at the moment. Odd-looking spines

appeared in his fluff, but very quickly unfurled into beautiful feathers.

It was incredible how fast the fluff was going. Great blobs of it wafted into the air every time he moved and though he didn't look so sweet any more, Solomon was dying for him to learn to fly.

In the evening William Oakley phoned Miss Birkett. Only hearing half a conversation, Solomon couldn't understand much.

William Oakley rumpled Solomon's hair almost the same way as he had stroked the dying dog. "We've got a fight on our hands," he growled. Then he just looked despairing. "It's no good, though. I don't think they'll let us."

"A fight?" For a moment Solomon couldn't think what Oakley meant. "You mean Miss Birkett – and Social Services? Because you told them a lie? Can't you just tell them what you told me? That you did it because you wanted me? And Sonia didn't any more."

"I did. I told them everything."

"But why won't they?"

"There's much more to it than that. These days adoption is a very difficult matter. Very few babies come up for adoption – there are far more parents wanting babies than babies wanting parents. Even with older children you've got to be pretty well perfect to succeed.

"There's been so much in the papers about social workers making mistakes, and children having a bad time. Oh, I know they mustn't let children go to the wrong people. That would be terrible." He picked up an old magazine and scrunched it up angrily, then flung it across the room.

"I don't want anyone perfect. I want … you," Solomon said.

"Mmm." Oakley smiled hopelessly. "You see, Sonia and I applied for adoption together. Without Sonia I'm a single man. And Social Services don't like single men to adopt."

He threw up his hands. "She said they would discuss it, but she didn't hold out much hope. Sonia left me single – and without Sonia they won't do it."

Chapter 20

Solomon took Barney on his arm and wandered out into the fields alone. It seemed pointless going for a walk without Josie, so after a bit he just sat down and let Barney hop around beside him.

All around, insects buzzed and small animals rustled in the long grass. Barney was wide awake, cocking his head to every sound, eyes picking on every movement. Suddenly he shot forward and plucked a fat grasshopper from a leaf. Solomon laughed at his happy surprise, as he gobbled it up with squishy crunching noises.

Then despair hit Solomon in full. He had just got Barney. He had just found how much he wanted to stay with William Oakley. Was it all to be finished?

Solomon knew there was no fight: Miss Birkett and the Social Services were stronger than him and William Oakley. Miss Birkett had said his case was "being discussed". He knew the authorities better than Oakley did. It was her way of saying "No". And it was all supposed to be for his own good – for him, Solomon.

"I hope – I hope Miss Bucket gets BSE," he said bitterly to Barney, flicking away a fly which was trying to land on his hair. Barney wasn't listening; he was more interested in the fly. His head circled as the fly circled Solomon's head

"And", Solomon added, "you ought to take more notice of what's going to happen to you. Mr Cluff is nice, but he won't have time to take you out like this."

And it's just because stupid Sonia went away. What's so bad about a single man? he thought.

Suddenly Solomon jumped up. The fly whizzed off; Barney gave a cross snort and

ruffled his feathers sulkily. Solomon picked him up. Barney nibbled him on the wrist – rather hard – but Solomon didn't notice.

"Barney," he said, "I think I've got it!" Barney blinked. "It's the answer to all our problems! It's been staring us in the face," Solomon told him.

Barney shut his eyes and went to sleep. Solomon smiled. "Silly twit, Barney." But Barney was dead to the world.

Solomon thought through his idea: if he wasn't allowed to stay with William Oakley because Oakley was single – well then, he'd better find Oakley a wife.

Just think – he'd be able to help choose his own mother. For once, being an orphan had a real advantage. Most people grumbled like anything about their parents; he would be choosing his own! It was a brilliant solution. So, yah boo sucks to stupid old Miss Bucket! The day seemed bright after all. With a still sleeping Barney on his arm, Solomon set off for the cottage.

For the moment, Solomon decided not to tell William. He set his mind to work.

The first woman Solomon thought of was a girl who worked at the Post Office. He had often noticed her when he went to buy Oakley's paper or some milk there – she was always friendly, and quite pretty, with red hair and large green eyes.

He went to check her out. Skulking behind a pillar hung with cards of hairgrips and needles, he picked up some useful information. She was not married; she lived with her sister in a flat nearby. (So there was a sister – another possibility if this one didn't work out.) And her name was Rosie – a lovely name. Solomon wouldn't mind a mother called Rosie.

Rosie had forgotten there was anyone else in the shop. She pulled out a small mirror and repaired her make-up. She puffed up her lips and admired them. Then she held the mirror further away and watched herself making kissy-kissy faces.

Solomon found this rather embarrassing. He supposed William might like that sort of thing, but he wished the pillar was a bit less narrow. He wished someone else would come into the shop.

Rosie put away the mirror. Then she wrinkled up her pretty nose and began to pick it. Solomon picked his own nose; seeing someone else do it was different. But Rosie hadn't finished yet. She got a nice gluey bit, admired it – and popped it in her mouth.

With a loud clatter, Solomon left.

Well, that was that as far as Rosie the Post Office girl went. Who else was there? The cowman's daughter smelt of cows. What about the neighbour with the cat? Carrie Bolsover was a bit old, but very jolly – then

Solomon remembered that Barney wouldn't like the cat, even if it did catch mice for him.

Then he hit on it: Jackie, the waitress at the restaurant. She'd be perfect! He pictured William and himself sitting in the kitchen at Screech Cottage, Jackie bustling to and fro with plates full of cakes – or maybe even leftovers from the restaurant trolley.

Solomon's mouth watered at the very thought. He remembered how jokey she was. It would be fun with Jackie as his mother. She had shining hair and a lovely face. How could William Oakley do anything but fall straight in love?

Chapter 21

The next problem was how to make it all happen. And he had very little time. Miss Birkett said he must leave at the end of the week. Solomon begged for a few more days, and luckily she gave in.

William Oakley couldn't bear to speak to Miss Birkett. He couldn't understand why Solomon was so cheerful all of a sudden. In the short time they had left, he wanted to do everything he could to please him.

Solomon said, "I think we should have a dinner party."

William Oakley looked startled. "A dinner party?" Somehow it wasn't the kind of thing he expected a boy of Solomon's age to want.

"A really posh one. Candles and a table-cloth. That sort of thing."

"I can't cook."

"We needn't do anything hard."

Oakley scratched his head. He wasn't too keen on the idea, but if it was what Solomon really wanted... "Who can we invite?" he said reluctantly.

Solomon tried to sound casual. "Well, people like that nice woman at the restaurant ... now what was her name – Jackie."

"Jackie? Very beautiful. Who else?"

"She'll do," Solomon said hastily. "It might get a bit complicated if we have too many."

"Just her? But I hardly know her!"

Solomon produced the little packet of matches he'd picked off the restaurant table. "Look, you've got the number right here."

"Um ... isn't there anything else you'd rather do?" William said weakly.

Solomon's face turned sadder and more orphan-like than Oakley had ever seen before. "I've never had a dinner party before. They don't have dinner parties in the Home."

William Oakley drooped into a chair. "This

place is filthy. We'll have to clean it up a bit."

Solomon's eyes lit up. "You mean she's coming?"

William Oakley nodded gloomily. Then he remembered. That Jackie was Quite Something.

Chapter 22

Barney grew up a lot that week. Already his wings were feathery enough to raise him from his perch – but not to lift him into the air. Barney would end up upside down, flapping madly and clinging to his perch for dear life. His face would twiddle round this way and that as if he was confused about which way up he really should be. It didn't seem to put him off, for five minutes later he did exactly the same thing again.

Every day you could see his wing-muscles were getting stronger. He spent a lot of time hopping to higher and higher objects and spreading his wings to sail down. In fact, he was very nearly flying properly.

Solomon saw this with a mixture of pride

and fear. He just had to get this wife thing right. It was their only chance.

Solomon looked round. The house (more or less) sparkled. They had moved the kitchen table into the sitting room. It now wore a red cloth and long white candles. A vase of pink and blue flowers sat on the dresser. Solomon thought it looked really smart. But would Jackie like it?

"Is the … stew thing all right?" he asked.

The stew was a bit of a cheat. William was a hopeless cook. He couldn't think what to do.

In despair they asked Carrie Bolsover. Carrie had been only too happy to help.

"A stew'll be the easiest," she'd said. "You buy the ingredients and I'll do it for you. It'll be a little thank-you for all those nasty mice you've taken away."

"The stew's fine," Oakley told Solomon. "I've just checked it. It's got masses of wine in. Should be good."

William had shaved till his chin squeaked: Solomon was making him nervous. "Baked potatoes are in. And both salads done."

"I'll just go and see my mousse again," Solomon said. "See if it's set." It had.

The stew might be a cheat, but the mousse was every bit Solomon's work. Solomon had got the recipe from a TV programme and it had taken ages. You were expected to help cook at the Home, but that was just whippy stuff out of packets. This was different – all those eggs – and real chocolate. He decorated it carefully with cream and sprinkled chocolate strands on top. It looked beautiful.

"Better shut Barney out," William said.

Solomon agreed reluctantly: he thought it

looked as if a storm were brewing. He didn't want Barney to be scared and alone in the aviary, so he sneaked upstairs and left him in his bedroom.

Jackie arrived just before the first rain. She looked stunning. And William (to Solomon's satisfaction) looked stunned.

"Hiiiii!" said Jackie warmly. Her hair was loose and every time she flicked it back it moved in a golden wave. Her red dress clung to her in glossy wrinkles. Solomon wondered how she could walk in such high heels. He was very glad he'd remembered to brush the dog hairs from the chair she was sitting on.

William gulped. "Er ... hello."

Jackie looked round. "Where's everybody else?"

"We-ell..." began William.

Solomon thrust a bowl of crisps at her. They were a new kind, called "Sofisto's". The packet said they were "sweet'n'sour salmon flavour".

"Mmm. Interesting," Jackie said.

"Interesting," they all agreed.

Outside, the storm broke; lightning flashed and an angry wind tore at the trees, drumming twigs at the window.

"My, I'm glad to be out of that!" Jackie smiled.

Inside it was warm and comfortable. Solomon lit the candles and the room took on a soft glow. He kept looking at William: was he in love yet? He must be. William seemed tongue-tied. Solomon decided it must be a good sign. Luckily, Jackie talked enough for both of them.

The prawn cocktail went down brilliantly. Jackie ate every bit, and admired the radish flowers Solomon had made.

Somewhere else in the house, a door blew open and a blast of cold air sent goose-pimples down their necks and nearly snuffed the candles.

Jackie chattered on. William was waiting for her to stop, so he could go and see where that draught was coming from.

Solomon wasn't listening. He thought he could hear somebody in the kitchen. Or was it the wind?

135

Suddenly Jackie's jaw dropped. "What's that!"

"Barney!" cried Solomon. "You're flying!"

Barney flew in lopsided – he wasn't too good at it yet. He missed Solomon's shoulder and crash-landed on the table. He sat there, hissing crossly.

William threw an annoyed look at Solomon. Solomon looked guilty. He couldn't have shut his bedroom door properly. Inside he was fizzing with excitement: he wanted to jump up and leap about, but he knew he shouldn't

at a dinner party. Barney flying at last!

William was excited, too, though he wished Barney hadn't chosen the dinner party for his first flight.

Barney began to walk up and down on the table, snorting to himself softly and looking round the room. Every now and then he lowered his head and glared at Jackie.

But worse was to come. Upset by the flickering candles, Barney tried to take off again. This time his sharp claws caught in the tablecloth. He flapped wildly, but, however

hard he tried, he was caught fast. He let out a scream of anger and fear.

Jackie jumped up in terror. "Take it away — don't let it get me!" she cried.

Barney rose with the tablecloth still attached. Knives and forks clattered to the floor and a wine glass smashed. William rescued the candles and blew them out.

Barney was caught and put safely away in his old box in the outhouse. But the damage was done. The evening was spoiled. Stew was put in front of them, but none of them ate much. William hardly said a word.

William brought the mousse in.

"Ooh! Doesn't it look lovely!" Jackie cried.

"It's the first time I've made one," Solomon said. "I did it all myself." He was cheered. Maybe the evening could be saved after all?

"Cream, chocolate vermicelli and — how clever — a chocolate truffle." She seemed very impressed.

"Chocolate truffle?" William looked at Solomon.

"But I didn't put a chocolate truffle on," Solomon said.

"Look, there it is," Jackie said. She peered closer. Then she sniffed. "It – it doesn't smell quite…" Her voice trailed away.

Solomon and William exchanged glances. What they were looking at was certainly not a chocolate truffle. It was an owl pellet.

"Erm…" William tried to think of something to say, but couldn't.

Jackie wouldn't listen to any explanation. Mumbling something about "a sudden headache", she left.

Chapter 23

The storm tore on. It was a wild night. "Oh well," William said.

They sat, gloomily surrounded by the wreckage of the destroyed evening. Solomon was miserable. Far better than William, he knew that with Jackie gone, his idea and all his hopes had failed. Now there was very little chance of being adopted.

All Solomon's excitement about Barney flying had vanished with her. Barney flying meant he was grown up, quite old enough to live with Mr Cluff.

William could fight Miss Birkett off for another week, two weeks, but at the end of it Solomon would have to leave. Time had run out.

Solomon fetched Barney in. He held him on his hand and stroked the springy feathers. Barney twiddled his head round and nibbled Solomon gently under his chin with a friendly burbling sound.

"Poor old clever Barney. You were terrified." Suddenly Barney flew up with a squeal. A minute later there was a small noise at the door. It was hard to hear beneath the sound of the storm.

The noise came again. It sounded like a timid knock.

William got up to see.

Standing on the doorstep was Miss Birkett. She looked like nothing on earth. Her hair stuck to her face in sodden strings, each one dripping its own river down her neck and making her smudged lipstick look even more peculiar than usual. Her flowery dress was torn and covered in mud. She was shivering with cold.

"You'd better come in," said William.

"I'm sorry," Miss Birkett said. "I'm ruining your floor. Perhaps—" But whatever "perhaps" she had in mind vanished under the weight of her troubles. Her lip wobbled, and though she bit it hard to try and stop herself, she burst into tears.

Both Solomon and William instantly forgot everything else but trying to comfort her.

"It doesn't matter about the floor. Come into the kitchen – it's warmer there," William said. To Solomon, he said, "Go and run a bath. Miss Birkett looks freezing."

"Oh, Jenny, please," mumbled Miss Birkett. "You're being so kind – and you must hate me so much." Solomon and William looked away.

"I must tell you – before anything. I was coming to warn you – only my car broke down – miles away and—" She sniffed loudly. Solomon handed her a tissue.

"It was dark. I walked miles and miles. For ages I thought I was lost – and – branches kept falling – one fell right across my path." She was pale and shivering at the memory.

"You're safe now," William said. "How about that bath?"

Miss Birkett shook her head. "No, I must tell you everything first. It's my boss and the area supervisor. They've made a final decision on Solomon. They say he's got to go back to the Home."

She looked at Solomon, then at William. "They've got a silly bee in their bonnets about single men not being suitable to adopt. I've been telling them for ages that I thought you two were right for each other." She gave a wry smile. "That day your dog died — I know I was in the way, but I had to be sure. They'd been on and on about getting you back. I didn't want to push you in case I was wrong — but I could see you were beginning to click."

"Only we didn't say so," said William.

"It was my fault. I was a bit slow," Solomon said.

Miss Birkett smiled. "It made it much harder." She hesitated. "There's something else. I also came to say goodbye. You see, I've resigned from my job."

"What? You've given up your job because of us?" William said.

Miss Birkett nodded. "Well, I wasn't very good at it — but I do know they're wrong about your case. I told them they were sexist," she said with a twinge of mischief. "They didn't like that."

She shivered. William sent her up to her bath.

When Miss Birkett came down, she looked quite different. Without that lipstick on she looked fresh and glowing. And in a funny way, the enormous old jumper William had lent her, suited her.

"Do you know, I suddenly feel hungry," William said. "There's masses of food left. And stew's always better second time round." He put it back in the oven. He seemed very cheerful all of a sudden.

Solomon suddenly noticed the way William was looking at Miss Birkett – his eyes were glazed and he was wearing the most ridiculous soppy smile.

"I'll give you a lift home later. But you'll stay for something to eat first – Jenny?"

Jenny Birkett blushed. "Nothing could be nicer."

They told her about the messed-up evening, and how awful it was finding an owl pellet in the chocolate mousse and she laughed so hard she almost cried again.

"Would it be too dreadful to scrape off the top bit?" she said. "It does seem wicked to waste something so good."

Without a word, Solomon lit the candles again. A wonderful, marvellous thought was growing in his mind. It was so unexpected, and so good it tingled him all down his spine.

William was about to shoo Barney from the room, but Miss Birkett said, "Oh no, do let him stay. He'll get used to the candles in a moment. It wouldn't be the same without him."

She watched Barney with her head on one side. "He's male, isn't he? He hasn't got many spots."

She knows! thought Solomon. She knows about owls.

As Solomon went to get the delicious stew from the oven, he thought that perhaps, after all, everything was going to be all right. Behind him, William and Jenny Birkett were chattering away like happy budgerigars. He stood still and listened for a bit. He couldn't

pick out words, but he guessed the expression on Jenny Birkett's face was every bit as soppy as William's.

Solomon had the oven gloves in his hand when William appeared at the door. "Need any help?" William said loudly. He beckoned Solomon and hissed. "I've just had this amazing idea… You see, if Jenny and—"

"I know." Solomon smiled.

William looked at him anxiously. "Well?"

"Brilliant," Solomon whispered. Aloud he said, "Just coming – you go back."

"Jenny…" He tried it out. Or "Mum". Which would it be? They sounded as mouth-watering as the stew on his tongue. Never mind, there would be plenty of time to decide all that…

Outside, the storm was over. A fearsome scream rippled into the rain-clean air. Barney cocked his head to listen.